Book 1

Life in the Neck
New Friends

Written by
Diane Davies

Illustrated by
Margarita Sikorskaia

BEAVER'S
POND
PRESS

Always be friendly and kind.
— Diane Davies

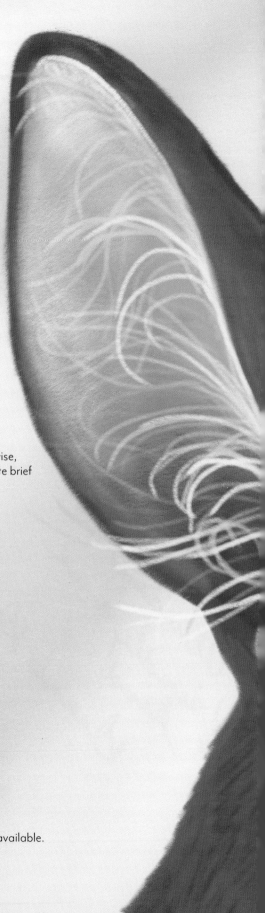

To my grandchildren, Elsie and Eli.
Always remember to treat your friends
as you would like them to treat you!
This book is also dedicated to Piper, in memory.
—DD

To my mother Lydia,
who strongly encouraged me
to develop my talents.
—MS

Edited by Alicia Ester
Illustrated by Margarita Sikorskaia

ISBN: 978-1-59298-690-3
Library of Congress Catalog Number: 2018905515
Printed in the United States of America
First Printing: 2018
22 21 20 19 18   5 4 3 2 1

Cover and interior design by Sara J Weingartner

BEAVER'S
POND
PRESS

Beaver's Pond Press, Inc.
7108 Ohms Lane
Edina, MN 55439-2129

(952) 829-8818
www.BeaversPondPress.com

To order, visit www.ItascaBooks.com or call (952) 345-4488. Reseller discounts available.

For classroom ideas and teaching suggestions, visit **www.DianeDavies.com**.

Chapter 1: Delaney

Big brown eyes blinked open for the first time,
taking in the beauty of the brown eyes
looking right back at her.

"Mother?" asked the new fawn.
"Are you my mother?"

"Yes, little one. Your name is Delaney and I've been waiting for you. Welcome to life in the Neck," said Mother Deer. "You have a lot to learn before the cold wind comes, but for now, just rest. I'll teach you when you grow stronger."

"But . . . but . . . but . . . what's a neck?" squealed the curious fawn. "I want to see! What is the cold wind?"

"The Neck is a long, narrow strip of land that runs along the river. We call it our home. Now rest," answered Mother Deer. "You will know the cold wind when it arrives."

"But . . . but . . . but . . . what are we?"

"We are whitetail. Shhhhh. Rest, I said," ordered the new mom.

"But . . . but . . . but . . . what are white tails? I just have to know!" begged Delaney.

"We are whitetail deer. Lift up your little tail for me. Do you see how it is covered in white fur underneath?"

Delaney lifted her tail. "Wow, that sure is pretty," she giggled. "But . . . but . . . but . . . why is it there?"

"Oh my! You are full of questions. Lifting up your white tail like a flag is a warning to the other deer that you have found danger."

"But . . . but . . . but . . . what's danger?"

"You'll have plenty of time to learn about danger in the weeks ahead. Now rest, my sweet little one. Tomorrow is another day with many more lessons."

The new fawn grew in strength and understanding over the next weeks as promised. Delaney kept asking questions, learning daily from Mother Deer's answers.

On a trip across the drive to forage (find plants to eat), Delaney had her first brush with real danger. Mother Deer suddenly stopped and the little fawn ran right into her back legs.

"Oops!" giggled Delaney.

"Shhh," came Mother Deer's sharp reply. Her nose and ears went straight up in the air.

"Lay down, Delaney. Now! Close your eyes and be very, very still."

Delaney did as she was told. She opened her eyes just a peek as she saw Mother Deer lift her tail and dart away from where Delaney was hidden in the corn.

Old Coyote came out of the woods and chased Mother Deer. The other deer saw her warning as she sprinted into the woods, drawing the predator away from his prey, Delaney.

After losing her, Old Coyote tired quickly and walked unhappily back into the forest. He'd have to settle for a Canadian goose for his lunch.

Mother Deer found Delaney just as she had left her. "What a good listener you are. I'm so proud of you for following directions. The danger is gone now."

"But . . . but . . . but . . . what was chasing you? I saw your flag up," whimpered Delaney. "Was that the cold wind?"

"Come, I'll tell you on the way home!" replied Mother Deer, relieved they were both safe.

Chapter 2: Rocket

As a new day began, Rocket, a young cottontail rabbit who lived in an empty woodchuck burrow, set out to play.

Born that spring, Rocket was now nearly full grown at just three months of age. Like Delaney, he had a tail white on its underside. It was called a cottontail. But it was his special ears, not his tail, that kept him from danger.

When predators like eagles and hawks came near, Mother Rabbit heard and hurried her family into their safe burrow. Rocket learned well from her. His speed and excellent hearing had saved him many times.

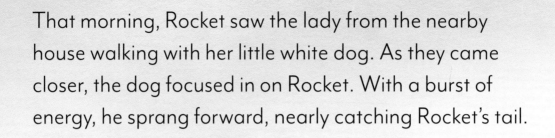

That morning, Rocket saw the lady from the nearby house walking with her little white dog. As they came closer, the dog focused in on Rocket. With a burst of energy, he sprang forward, nearly catching Rocket's tail.

Rocket's strong back legs sent him toward the cornfield with the dog close behind. Just as Rocket reached the corn, he turned, flying back across the drive. The dog ran straight into the corn while Rocket picked up speed and headed for the safety of a fallen tree's branches.

Rocket giggled. "Come on, dog! That was so fun.
Let's do it again. I know you can't catch me."

Coming out of the corn, the dog lost interest.

Mother Deer had sent Delaney out into the forest to look for food. As she skipped along, she came nose to nose with Rocket.

"But . . . but . . . but . . . what are you?" Delaney asked.

"I'm a cottontail rabbit," Rocket replied. "You sure are pretty."

"Thank you! But . . . but . . . but . . . what do you do?" asked Delaney.

"I like to hop and run around. Come play with me. Let's be friends."

The two new pals headed off into the brush. When they stopped to eat, Delaney saw Rocket use his nose to move food in front of his paws.

"I keep all of my feet on the ground when I eat, just like you do. But can't you use your front paws to put food in your mouth?" she asked.

"No," said Rocket. "I use my nose to move the food to where my mouth can reach it. I can use my paws to bring down the good stuff above me, but that's all."

"I can reach up high with my mouth and get some really good leaves for you. Would that be okay?"

"Sure," replied Rocket. "Friends help each other. Thanks."

Mother Deer and Mother Rabbit were close by, enjoying the sight of the two new friends playing. Another set of eyes was watching too.

Mother Rabbit heard the coyote first as he moved in closer to Delaney and Rocket. Mother Deer grunted to warn Delaney of the nearby danger. Then everyone moved all at once. Delaney and Mother Deer lifted their tails and dashed away. Rocket and Mother Rabbit scurried into the woods and down their burrow. Old Coyote was left licking his chops. Another day, another Canadian goose lunch.

"But . . . but . . . but . . . what just happened?" cried Delaney. "Was that the cold wind?"

"The old coyote was watching you from the woods. You were too busy playing to see him. You must be careful at all times, my sweet little one," Mother Deer said.

Chapter 3: Cardinal Red

"Whoit, whoit, whoit! What-cheer, what-cheer," called Cardinal Red, the first of the songbirds to sing in the new day in the Neck.

"Hey, hey, hey," shouted Delaney to the crested songbird. "I love your singing! Do you want to be friends?"

"Hey, hey, hey, little fawn. I've been watching you grow for many weeks now. I will gladly be your friend."

"Yay!" replied Delaney. "Would you like to meet my friend Rocket and be his friend too?"

"Of course! I've seen you playing together and helping each other find food. I've also watched that Old Coyote fella. Be careful or he will have you for lunch."

Cardinal Red and his wife lived in the old oak tree at the beginning of the drive. Their nest of vines, twigs, and leaves was built up high in the tree. The reddish-brown color of Cardinal Red's wife made it easy for her to stay hidden while she sat on their three eggs, guarding them from hawks, squirrels, and owls. Their babies would hatch soon. Then Cardinal Red would need to find seeds, fruit, and worms to feed his family.

"Rocket and I found the people's garden down at the bottom of the hill. Want us to show you where it is so you can find food when the babies hatch?" Delaney asked Cardinal Red.

Excited to share, the three friends headed happily to the garden plot. The people had planted carrots, lettuce, green beans, tomatoes, and radishes. The garden was overgrown with pumpkin vines and quack grass, providing seeds, fresh green leaves, and vines. The variety gave all three good things to eat.

The afternoon slipped away as they ate their fill and began to feel sleepy in the warm sun. Their eyes soon closed.

As they slept, a large bird circled above their heads. Feeling its shadow before she saw it, Delaney's eyes popped open.

"Hey, hey, hey, Cardinal Red. Wake up, wake up!" cried Delaney. "That hawk is robbing the Neck. Fly home to save your nest!"

Cardinal Red flew off toward the old oak while the others dove into the shelter of the pumpkin plants' great leaves to hide from the danger.

Old Coyote watched from his hiding spot in the forest. He and Hawk would both have Canadian goose for lunch that day.

Chapter 4: The Cold Wind of Danger

Early September found the Neck very, very dry.
No rain had fallen for the last three weeks.
The chance of fire was high.

One morning, before the sun was even up,
a careless stranger threw a glowing
cigarette butt out of his car.

Landing in the tinder dry grass along the drive, it burst into flames. He didn't see them crawl across the grass to climb a nearby tree. A cold wind blew, fanning them even higher until the open wood at the beginning of the Neck was full of fire.

Sitting high up in the old oak, Cardinal Red was the first to notice the danger.

"Whoit, whoit, whoit!" he shrieked to warn the other animals. He flew over the area, spreading the alarm. He was happy to see the whitetail deer escaping with their tails held high. The cottontail rabbits hurried to the safety of the grassland downwind. The squirrels, chipmunks, foxes, songbirds, snakes, turtles, and frogs followed the rabbits out of the fire's path.

Cardinal Red was proud of his fine warning until he saw that Delaney and Rocket were missing. The fire grew as the wind pushed it along the Neck toward the end of the drive.

"The garden!" screeched Cardinal Red. Surely that was where he would find Delaney and Rocket. Cardinal Red flew harder and faster than he ever had before.

Rocket spotted Cardinal Red and called, "Delaney is hiding and won't come out!"

Old Coyote was once again watching. He knew the roaring fire was making its way toward the frightened fawn. He also knew Delaney believed she was safe as long as she lay very still and waited for Mother Deer to come get her. But Delaney's mother could not save her this time. He quickly and quietly made his way to where Delaney was hidden.

Delaney looked up, right into Old Coyote's eyes. "Run, run, Delaney! Your mother is waiting for you in the grassland. Now run, run as fast as you can!" shouted Old Coyote.

Heart pounding, she jumped up and ran past him. The other animals followed, with Cardinal Red flying in the lead. Even Old Coyote raced with them to the grassland.

Thanks to Cardinal Red, the animals of the Neck were safe. Three new baby birds popped their heads above the nest when Cardinal Red returned. They had hatched just in time to welcome home their heroic dad.

Old Coyote waited until he saw Delaney and Rocket with their families and then snuck off into what was left of the Neck's woods, happy he had helped save his new friends. Once again he would have a Canadian goose lunch. And he was just fine with that!